Missing Violet

by
KELLY SWEMBA

illustrated by
FABIANA FAIALLO

beaming ☀ books
MINNEAPOLIS

Violet was my best friend and an expert at spreading sunshine. Her healing hugs made falls hurt less.

Games were more fun because Violet invited others to join.
And when I felt like drawing, Violet drew with me.

But something changed.
And one day, Violet went home sick.

Without her, I drew by myself.

I didn't have anyone to share jokes with at lunch.

And at reading buddy time, I was one buddy short.

One night, I called Violet.
She was very sick.
I tossed and turned all night, wondering how I could help.

The next day, I took action.
This has to work.
But . . .
her desk was still empty, while my stomach was full of butterflies.

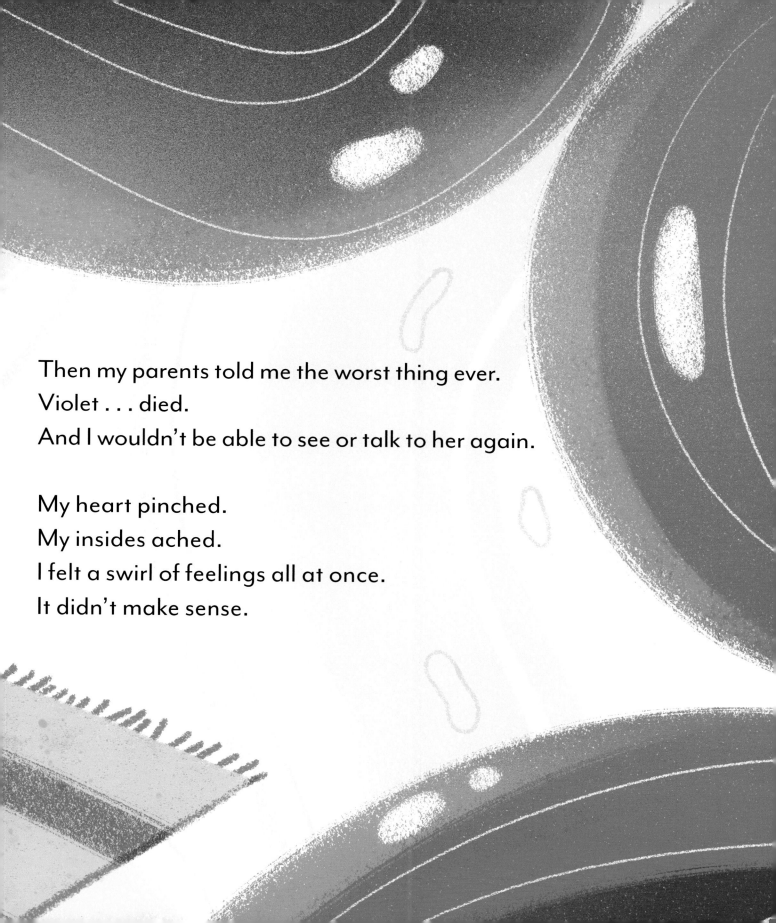

Then my parents told me the worst thing ever.
Violet . . . died.
And I wouldn't be able to see or talk to her again.

My heart pinched.
My insides ached.
I felt a swirl of feelings all at once.
It didn't make sense.

How could this happen—she's my best friend!
I clutched the heart necklace Violet gave me.
Who would share the other half now?

I felt odd—like an orange without its peel.

I scowled as classmates laughed and played. Why did THEY still get to be with their best friends?

I sizzled red hot as fire.
I thundered down the halls
and snapped at everyone.

I dragged through my days, feeling blue.
I started visiting the counselor.

She was nice—
but I still missed Violet.
And I missed feeling like me.

I wished things could be like before . . .
when I had a best friend to share my secrets with.
Someone who laughed at my jokes during lunch.
A friend who was always there.

I missed being with Violet and seeing her smiling face.
Wait—that's it!

I asked Mom for help.
Together, we printed pictures of Violet and me together.
We decorated a special box to put them in.
But tears rolled down my cheeks.

I stared out my window as rain drizzled down.
Then, through the clouds, something shimmered.

The rainbow wrapped the sky in a hug.
Just like Violet did for me when I was hurt.
I knew what to do.

The next day when someone fell during recess, I helped them up.
When a game started, I asked others to join.

And during reading time, I shared my story with someone new.
Sometimes I'd talk to my classmates about Violet.
Turns out, we ALL felt sad and missed her.
Then we had an idea.

Together, we wrote notes to Violet . . .
of things we wanted to tell her.
What we liked about her.
And what we missed.

Together, we said goodbye to our friend.

I still miss Violet.

On those days, I look for a rainbow . . .
and remember my friend.

A Note for Parents, Teachers, and Caregivers

Death is a difficult topic to discuss with children. Each child's knowledge of death is different. Start the conversation by asking about their feelings, thoughts, and ideas about death. This will help you understand what they still need to learn or what questions they have.

Be honest during the conversation. Avoid using phrases like "they've passed," "they're sleeping," or "they went on a long trip." These will only confuse and potentially scare the child. Be gentle and allow time for them to process their emotions and what they're experiencing.

Children often express emotion through play and art. Invite them to draw their feelings. Listen attentively when they play, in case something important is said.

Children sometimes worry that they will forget the person who died. Help them make a memory box filled with pictures and stories.

Another activity is to make a memory chain. Make strips of paper, write or draw a memory on each strip, and then make a chain, linking each memory to another. This chain can be hung in a classroom or in your child's room. It can be a helpful reminder of the good times they shared together.

Though there are stages of grief, everyone experiences them differently. There isn't a set order or time frame for this process. If you feel concerned, please reach out to your pediatrician or school counselor for support and guidance.

Further Reading

Elyse C. Salek and Kenneth R. Ginsbery, "How Children Understand Death and What You Should Say," HealthyChildren.org, September 11, 2014, https://www.healthychildren.org/English/healthy-living/emotional-wellness/Building-Resilience/Pages/How-Children-Understand-Death-What-You-Should-Say.aspx.

David J. Schonfeld and Marcia Quackenbush, "After a Loved One Dies: How Children Grieve and How Parents and Other Adults Can Support Them," New York: New York Life Foundation, 2014, https://www.newyorklife.com/assets/docs/pdfs/claims/Bereavement-bklet-English.pdf.

"Helping Kids Grieve," Sesame Street in Communities, accessed March 7, 2022, https://sesamestreetincommunities.org/topics/grief/.

For my loves Michael, Katelyn, and Owen.
Thank you for coloring my world with everything beautiful.—KS

To my niece Manuela and my nephew Enrico,
who love to hear good stories.—FF

28 27 26 25 24 23 22   1 2 3 4 5 6 7 8

Hardcover ISBN: 978-1-5064-8331-3
eBook ISBN: 978-1-5064-8332-0

Names: Swemba, Kelly, author. | Faiallo, Fabiana, illustrator.
Title: Missing Violet / by Kelly Swemba ; illustrated Fabiana Faiallo.
Description: Minneapolis, MN : Beaming Books, 2023. | Includes
  bibliographical references. | Audience: Ages 5-8. | Summary: When Mia's
  best friend Violet gets sick and does not recover, Mia works through the
  stages of grief like the colors of the rainbow. Includes a note for
  parents, teachers, and caregivers.
Identifiers: LCCN 2022026653 (print) | LCCN 2022026654 (ebook) | ISBN
  9781506483313 (hardcover) | ISBN 9781506483320 (ebook)
Subjects: CYAC: Grief--Fiction. | LCGFT: Picture books.
Classification: LCC PZ7.1.S935 Mi 2023 (print) | LCC PZ7.1.S935 (ebook) |
  DDC [E]--dc23
LC record available at https://lccn.loc.gov/2022026653
LC ebook record available at https://lccn.loc.gov/2022026654

VN0004589; 9781506483313; DEC2022

Beaming Books
PO Box 1209
Minneapolis, MN 55440-1209
Beamingbooks.com

KELLY SWEMBA has been passionate about big feelings since she was little. She holds a master's degree in psychiatric nursing and has also worked as a preschool intervention aide for children with autism. She's a member of SCBWI, 12x12, and Children's Book Insider. Kelly lives with her family in Columbus, Ohio.

FABIANA FAIALLO is a freelance illustrator who has done work for children's magazines, textbooks, and children's books. She was born and raised in Brazil, and still lives there today.